THE REVOLUTION

James Mitchum Oates

Author's Tranquility Press
Marietta, Georgia

James Mitchum Oates /Author's Tranquility Press
2706 Station Club Drive SW
Marietta, GA 30060
www.authorstranquilitypress.com

Publisher's Note: This is a work of fiction. Names, characters, places, and incidents are a product of the author's imagination. Locales and public names are sometimes used for atmospheric purposes. Any resemblance to actual people, living or dead, or to businesses, companies, events, institutions, or locales is completely coincidental.

Ordering Information:
Quantity sales. Special discounts are available on quantity purchases by corporations, associations, and others. For details, contact the "Special Sales Department" at the address above.

The Revolution/ James Mitchum Oates
Hardcover: 978-1-957208-18-3
Paperback: 978-1-957208-19-0
eBook: 978-1-957208-20-6

Table of Contents

Dedication

Thanks go to my publishing company – Author's

Tranquility Press.

And special thanks go to my family for all of the support.

Without you, this wouldn't be possible.

Introduction

What is racism and discrimination? It is something that, here in America, minorities experience on the average of many times in their life span. It overshadows the ideal of harmony and brotherhood in this country and causes many whites to hate blacks. This preconceived notion of racism and discrimination halts positive progression and defaces the idea of America as a melting pot.

Such a powerful force has to have roots or an origin. When looking up the definition of racism and discrimination in the dictionary, it does not define the core essence of this ideology. That core essence, plain and simple, is just a lack of knowledge. Racism and discrimination stem and grow from a lack of knowledge. Many whites who are racist towards blacks are so due to a lack of knowledge. And it is this lack of knowledge that gets replaced with lies and falseness that gives them their basis to hate blacks. This hatred then becomes inclusive to ALL blacks. Thus, you have the situation that arises of when a racist white person comes into contact with a black person, the hatred is there too and they don't even have to know this person – only their skin color.

This is part of the result of the ignorance that stereotypes breed. An ignorance set into the mind-set of an innocent child that does not know hatred based on color until this is what they're taught by their adult figures. And as that child gets older, the ignorance and hatred so grow with them until they too one day have children and their ideals are then instilled upon them and so on.

This cycle has been going on in this country since its inception. Another example is the story of the Native Americans. They inhabited this country long before white people even thought to come here. But when they did come, they slaughtered these people and took the land from them. But all throughout history, the media portrays in T.V. shows that cowboys are good and Indians are bad.

This negative and false portrayal feeds into the mind of the young and gives them false notions that they grow up with. And in this problem lies a large portion of the solution – through talking about and teaching the truth. We need more honest and open dialogue from whites and blacks together.

Can this happen in a timely fashion, or is it too late for America? The answer is it's never too late. But the sooner, the better. The longer we wait, the worse the conditions get and the more hatred spreads. We have the chance to act now while we have American values set and engraved in stone.

ONE

Roger could hear the girls outside playing jump rope occasionally saying, "It's my turn." As he sat on the living room floor with his brothers watching Ronald Reagan speak about eradicating crime in the urban communities, he suddenly recalled the passages from Dr. King's "I have a dream speech." It was almost time to begin reading more on the Civil Rights Movement and the techniques of non-violent action. His mother was in the kitchen just starting lunch.

"It's been over 25 years since the Civil Rights Movement and we as blacks still don't have what we're looking for in America," blurted out Chris the oldest brother.

"Yeah, that's why it's called a struggle. It's not supposed to happen over-night," interjected Jason the middle brother.

I tried to drown all of this out and listen to what the president had to say. But I kept getting distracted by the girls playing outside. That's where I should have been was outside. It was hot that day and it was going to get hotter.

Today was Saturday, and by it being so I could do what I enjoyed most—reading and studying of the black struggle in America. So after lunch, I went and caught the bus and went to the library. Of course, it was dangerous because of all of the gangs that hung out on the corners. Knowing the potential for danger in such an environment, why would my mom let me catch the bus under these conditions? The answer is she had an undying faith that God would always keep me safe. Here I was a fourteen-year-old young black man striving to receive knowledge – knowledge of my own people.

I was on the bus and feeling a bit anxious today because mom said I could stay at the library a couple of extra hours on this particular day. I gazed out of the window and wondered how I would divide my time studying so as to give an equal amount of time to each category I was studying. As I gazed out of the window, I was about to look away when I saw Smiley. Smiley was a very well-respected man in the community. He stood on the corner everyday handing out flyers and advertising for people to join "The Righteous Movement." What was "The Righteous Movement?" It was a group of believers who assembled together periodically to address the underlying issues in the community and ways of dealing with them in a positive manner. Its focus was on black awareness, the up-keep of the community, and changing the conditions for blacks from worse to better. This is where I needed to be. It was only a matter of time.

When I arrived at the library, I went right to the black history section. "Yep, there it is. Right where I left it." I pulled out the book I started reading last week. It was called, "The Troubles of the Light-Skinned Negro," by James Weldon Johnson. I opened the book where I had my bookmark placed, sat down at a table nearby and began to read. I was reading and reading and became so entranced and enthralled with the book, that before long, much time had passed and soon enough it was already time to go home. I couldn't believe how time flew!

When I got home, I went straight to bed. I wasn't hungry; only tired.

That night, I had the same reoccurring dream. I dreamed that my mom, brothers, me and my dad were in a restaurant eating. Suddenly, two white men stormed into the restaurant with guns waving them around and demanding money. Then they approached us and began saying derogatory things. They said, "Look at the monkeys eating. Do you want some fried chicken and potato salad you fucking niggers!" Mom then told dad not to be a hero. This is when dad tried to reason with the men. Then one of them shot daddy in the head point blank.

Why didn't you listen daddy?

I awakened to the sound of my mother calling me for breakfast. Even though I didn't eat dinner that night, I still wasn't hungry, but was still tired.

TWO

Mom made bacon, eggs, and toast for breakfast with orange juice to wash it all down with. In the middle of enjoying my breakfast, I heard mom scream, "Roger!" I very quickly, without thought, yelled, "Yes, ma'am."

I knew I had done something wrong. But what this time?

She then yelled, "What have I told you about leaving the toilet seat up when you're done?"

Then I became angry. Angry because it wasn't me! I didn't do it.

I looked at Jason, who was looking at me. He then shrugged and said, "I didn't do it." Then I looked at Chris. He was still eating. His constant munching on his bacon and avoidance from everything let me know it was him. I didn't make a big deal about it. I just let it go.

After breakfast, Jason and I did dishes. Then I walked to my room angry. Angry because of mom's false accusation. Then I thought to myself, "I wish Chris would own up to when he's wrong." I reached my room and closed the door and began making my bed. Shortly after I started, I thought to myself, "Chris be more accountable. Huh! That'll be the day."

After my room was cleaned and I had taken a nice hot bath and got dressed, I sat on my bed. It was almost time for me to start studying on more black history. I had scheduled myself for today to study on Marcus Garvey. But I had a sudden change of plans. My real interest lied in studying Dr. Martin Luther King Jr. I had already studied about him though. But I was fascinated with his life. His words were so powerful, they drew me to his speeches wanting to read more. But before I did that, I reached under my bed and pulled out my shoe box. I searched through all of the old pictures and papers until I found it. A picture of daddy. I held it and just looked at it for a while. His resemblance to me was undeniable. Then I reflected on the fact that it was this man who sparked my interest in black history and the black struggle. Six months ago, he was alive.

We miss you daddy.

Summer time was in and it was a scorcher. The good news is we were out of school. I would be starting high school in the fall. Jason the 10th, and Chris the 12th. This is where we were. South Central Detroit on 69th and Belleview.

"Mom, I'm going across the street to play basketball," I called out as I headed out the door. I hurried out with intentness for fear of mom calling me back telling me I couldn't go play because of an undone chore or something. I made it out and closed the door.

"Let's see, did I forget anything?"

"Nope. Alright then, it's off to the court."

When I got out there, I saw a bunch of older guys at one end of the court playing. Also, I saw a kid about my age at the other end of the court shooting hoops. I walked over to the older guys and asked them if I could join. They kept playing. Finally, one of them yelled, "Get outta here!" I walked away angry. Angry because I knew I was better than those guys. But because I was younger, they didn't want to give me a chance. Before I knew it, I was at the other end of the court.

The boy down there kept shooting hoops and ignored me for a little bit. Then, without looking at me, he asked, "Do you want to play HORSE?"

I loved this game and very quickly said, "Yes." He then said, "I'm Trevor."

I then said, "I'm Roger."

I had never seen this boy before in the area or at school. I asked, "You from around here?" Knowing he wasn't.

He then said, "I'm from North Carolina. My family moved up here last week."

He took the first shot from the side three-point lane. It went in.

I then said, "I was born here and I live in that building right there," pointing across the street. Then I took my shot from where he shot his. It went in too.

He then jokingly said, "I hope it's better here than in North Carolina," as he took his second shot from the opposite end of where he shot his first shot. It went in again.

I then quizzically asked, "Is it that bad in North Carolina? It can't be half as bad there as it is here." I then took my shot from where he shot his second shot. I missed this time.

He then said, "That's an 'H' for you."

He then asked, "Do you come out and play often?"

I then very proudly responded, "No, I spend a lot of my time at the library."

"What do you study?"

"I study a lot of black history and of Innovators and thinkers for the black struggle."

"Sounds pretty boring."

"Actually it's very interesting. I learn a lot of new stuff."

"Boring."

Soon I found myself rambling on and on with facts about black history and innovators of color and boring poor Trevor to death. Before long I realized that I had an "S" and Trevor only had an "O". He took his shot from the three-point lane and it went in. Then I shot and missed. I lost.

Then Trevor announced, "That's game."

We slapped hands and then he asked, "What are you doing tomorrow?"

Tomorrow I was scheduled to be at the library all day studying. I very excitedly replied, "I'm not doin' anything tomorrow," realizing that this was an invite to meet him here and play basketball again.

He then said, "Alright, tomorrow, same time?"

I confidently said, "I'll be here."

Then I turned around and crossed the street to go home. I stopped at the door and looked back. He was shooting more hoops. So I went in and closed the door.

That night, after dinner, I laid in bed in my room about to go to sleep. Then I thought about my new found friend.

I almost bored him to death today with all of the facts and figures I spouted out for him about black history. Then I thought, "It's not so bad." I was actually pleased to be so knowledgeable.

THREE

"Roger! Roger, honey, wake up!" I awakened to hear my mom saying while shaking me. I had the nightmare about daddy again. When would I forget?

Mom then said, "You were having another nightmare. Listen sweetie, you've got to think peaceful thoughts and those peaceful thoughts will carry on into your dreams. The ugly past is the ugly past. Let's focus on a bright future. God has so many positive things planned for you."

I then said, "Alright," and she left.

When she left, I lay there for a moment and thought of the soothing effect of mom's words. I then got up to eat breakfast.

When I walked into the kitchen, I was greeted with an aroma of eggs and bacon. Chris and Jason were already at the table. Mom was just getting ready to fix my plate.

"Well if it isn't Roger, the artful dodger."

"Leave me alone, Chris."

"Word of advice, when using the bathroom, put the toilet seat down first before you wash your hands. Reason being is you've already adapted to washing your hands before leaving the bathroom. Once you start putting the seat down before washing your hands, it'll become ingrained in your mind to put the seat down first and soon you'll do it without thought."

"Leave me alone, Chris!"

"Works for me," interjected Jason.

"Mom, can I be excused? I'm not very hungry today," I very meekly asked.

"No, not until you eat your breakfast," mom said, knowing I didn't want to be excused for a lack of hunger.

Suddenly, Chris got up and said, "Mom, I'm goin' over to Mike's house. I'll probably spend the night there, so don't wait up for me."

He then took two big gulps of orange juice from his glass and left. Somehow, after he left, my appetite came back.

After I washed my dishes, I went into the living room to watch T.V. Jason was already there sitting on the couch watching the news. I so badly wanted to turn to the cartoons. But I just decided to watch the news so as not to start anything.

The lady on T.V. then said, "In other news, more gang violence in the community leads to the death of two gang members last night in a shootout. Investigators have no suspects in custody."

Then I drifted off with the constant laughter and high shrills from the girls outside playing on the playground. Jason said something, but I didn't hear him. I was gone. I drifted deep into thought.

How safe are Chris, Jason, my mom and I here?

Why do things like this have to happen where we live?

Then I began to think about the teachings of non-violent action advocated by Dr. King.

How effective was this method anyway? Then I thought, "Seeing the conditions of today, not very effective."

Then his words came to me, "Brother, I may not get there with you, but I promise you that together as a people, we shall get to the Promiseland."

But when?

Shortly the news went off and Jason left and went elsewhere. This left me in total control of the T.V. But it was time for my studies. Although, today I figured to give it a break. I got up, went to my room, and laid on my bed. Before long, I was sleep. As I slept, I dreamed a peaceful dream. I dreamed that daddy, mom, Chris, Jason, and me were together in another city. We were all very happy with a decent amount of money. Daddy had a very successful business and mom stayed at home during the day. Chris had got accepted into a good college and Jason was following in his footsteps. Me, I was very happy with my studies and had access to the libraries to do my studies. Also, I had no fear of any gangs trying to hurt me because there were none. It was perfect. Then I woke up.

I awakened to an aroma of half-done potatoes—my favorite. Then I looked at my watch and it said 1:12 p.m. I was supposed to meet Trevor on the court at 1:00 p.m. I jumped out of bed and threw my shoes on and ran out of my room through the kitchen to the front door.

Mom then said, "Hey, hey, slow down. Where are you off to in such a hurry?"

"No time to talk, mom. I gotta meet my new friend on the court today and I'm already late."

"But don't you want some lunch? It's your favorite. Half-done potatoes."

"Sorry mom. Not now. I gotta go."

I closed the door behind me and ran down the stairs. I hoped Trevor hadn't left.

When I got outside, there he was, shooting hoops. I looked both ways before crossing the street, then darted across to the court. I ran up to him and said, "Hey!" He said, "What's up?" and we slapped hands.

"What's the word?"

"The word is 'freedom'."

"I hear you," he said. "Wanna play HORSE again?"

"Sure."

He got in the three-point lane and took his first shot. It went in. "So how do you know so much stuff about blackness?" he asked.

I then took my shot from where he shot. It went in.

"My dad used to make me study it all the time and it just kind-of stuck with me."

He took his second shot from another spot in the three-point lane. It went in again.

"I wished my dad cared that much about me. Your dad and my dad should meet and exchange qualities."

"That would be cool if it were possible, but my dad is dead."

I took my second shot from where he shot his. It missed.

"Sorry."

"That's alright. You didn't know."

"So how'd he die?"

He then took his third shot from another three-point spot. It went in.

I then started telling him how daddy died. Then I took my third shot. It missed again.

By the time I got done talking, I had an "S" and he didn't even have an "H". He shot his last shot. It went in. Then it was my turn. I missed again.

"That's 'HORSE'," he very triumphantly said. "Wanna play again?"

I didn't feel like playing anymore, so I said, "Naw, I'll sit this one out."

"Suit yourself," he said and continued shooting around. I took a seat on the pavement. It was hot that day and temperatures were supposed to rise that afternoon.

Yep, it was going to be one hot summer.

That evening, when I went home, Chris, Jason, and mom were there watching T.V. I went to my room and closed the door.

Later on, I came out for dinner, but first I had to wash my hands. I went in the bathroom and closed the door. Sure enough, the toilet seat was up. I wanted to leave it there for mom to see so Chris would get in trouble. Then I just decided to let it down.

No big deal.

Everyone was at the table and we were having cheeseburgers and fries. I loved cheeseburgers and fries and I was very hungry.

While we ate, Chris talked about how awesome he was at playing basketball today in Mike's backyard. He said a mouthful with his mouth full. I got so disgusted, I didn't want to eat. I excused myself from the table and went to my room and closed the door. I climbed into bed and before I went to sleep, I realized that I hadn't studied today. But it was too late now. I was already in bed and I wasn't getting up. I closed my eyes and went to sleep and hoped to dream about the cheeseburgers and fries I missed out on.

FOUR

Trevor proved to be a very great friend. Our only meetings were on the court, but we did a lot of talking. It was the middle of August, close to the end of summer and it was extremely hot. After we got done playing ball on this particular day, Trevor decided he wanted some ice cream. So we walked around the corner to the store to get some. As we walked and talked, suddenly, I saw Smiley about a half a block up passing out his flyers.

"What is that guy doing?"

"Oh, him? That's just Smiley passing out flyers."

"What are the flyers for?" asked Trevor as we approached Smiley.

"No Smiley, not today," I said dismissively as we walked by.

"He's been in this community for years handing out flyers and trying to recruit members for 'The Righteous Movement.'"

"The Righteous Movement?"

"Uh huh. It's a black awareness group."

"That sounds like where you need to be."

"Naw, not really."

"Why not? You spend enough time giving me knowledge of black history. You could certainly benefit from that group. You should get a flyer and look into it."

"Maybe when we come back."

When we finally got there, I was so pleased because I could hardly wait to indulge in my ice cream.

I very quickly marched up to the counter and said, "One cherry blossoms sugar cone please."

Then Trevor said, "And one orange sherbet sugar cone."

As the man prepared the cones, I began to dig in my pocket to pay for mine.

One problem – I left my money at home.

I began to get frustrated as I checked my back pockets, knowing nothing was there because I only put money in my front pockets. Trevor saw me digging and the frustration on my face and finally said, "Don't worry about it, bro. I've got you covered." He pulled out a few one dollar bills, gave them to the man, and we got our ice cream and left. I said, "Thanks," but he didn't know how grateful I really was.

On the way back, we weren't engaged in constant conversation as usual because we were too busy indulging in our cones. Talk about good!

About 3/4 of a block up, we saw Smiley again. This is when Trevor said, "You really oughta give it some thought."

I didn't really want to take a flyer as badly as he wanted me to. Although, he did buy your ice cream for you and you were extremely hot. Plus, you hadn't had lunch that day. Why not repay a favor with a favor?

When we got up to Smiley I said, "Smiley, I'll take one."

He looked kind-of surprised, but handed me one anyway. He then said, "Meetings are Tuesday and Thursday night at 7:00 p.m. at the old auditorium."

Finally, I could make myself known and let my voice be heard.

When we got back to the court, we decided not to play anymore, but just to chill. We were sitting on the ground and I was looking at the flyer when Trevor said, "I think you'd do great in a group like this. This is just what you need to bring you out." I agreed with Trevor wholeheartedly and right then and there decided to join. I couldn't wait to tell mom.

FIVE

"Well, I think it's a wonderful idea," said mom happily. "Just don't let it interfere with your school work. You know school starts soon."

"Alright," I said. We were sitting on the bed in her room at about 3:45 a.m. talking. I couldn't sleep because I was so excited about joining this group. I paced the floor in my room all night thinking about the possible doors this group could open up for me. Chris and Jason were still sleep.

"Now honey, I've got some good news for you too. I have a job interview on Tuesday. Isn't that great?"

"Yeah, it's wonderful. What kind of job is it?"

"It's a real estate consultant."

"Sounds pretty important."

"Well, one thing's for certain, it'll pay the bills."

"Good, cause I don't like being poor."

"You'll see, when I get this job, we'll live a lot better than what we have been living. Now honey, you should try and get some rest. I'm cooking a special lunch today to celebrate my new job."

That was something to look forward to. So I hopped up off her bed, said, "good night and thanks mom," and marched to my room to get some rest. When I got to my room to go to sleep, I didn't have a hard time at all falling asleep.

I woke up feeling fully rested and refreshed today. The aroma that greeted me was not of bacon and eggs, but of baked fish. I got up to go use the bathroom, then join everyone for breakfast. When I went into the bathroom, the first thing I saw was that the seat was up again. I knew who did it, but mom would think I did. So I used the restroom, let the seat down, and washed my hands and came out for breakfast.

It wasn't a big deal.

When I got to the table, I saw Jason eating baked fish, macaroni and cheese, and green peas. Chris must have already eaten and left.

I was going to enjoy this meal.

Mom was at the kitchen sink washing dishes when she turned and saw me standing in the doorway.

"Hey honey, you were resting so peacefully, I just decided to let you sleep. It's lunch time now. Hope you're hungry."

I quickly grabbed my chair, pulled it out, and sat down ready to indulge. Mom then came over and fixed my plate. I ate every bit, then asked for seconds.

On this particular day, I decided not to meet Trevor on the court, but to do a little studying and then focus on getting prepared for school. It was to start in two weeks, and though I was prepared physically with all of the supplies I needed, I didn't know if I were prepared mentally. One mental challenge I had to deal with was more or less an adjustment—with Chris.

Chris had been dating a girl for eight months now. The only problem was that she was white. He met her at school and they fell in love. Of course, this was a problem because she lived all the way across town well away from the urban community. But this didn't stop Chris. He would catch the bus all the way across town just to be with her. Neither her family, nor the whites in her community approved of this. They shouldn't be together.

Kind of like Romeo and Juliet.

But that didn't stop Chris. It just made him more anxious.

And me more afraid.

SIX

"Come on, Jason. I want to watch the cartoons. You always hog the remote," I pleadingly said.

"Nope, too bad," Jason very proudly responded. Chris was at his girlfriend's house again.

Suddenly, mom came flying through the front door and ran into the living room. Then she screamed, "I got the job!"

Jason and I both jumped up to hug her.

At that moment, the only thing I could think about was a better life for all of us.

"Mom, tonight is my first meeting for 'The Righteous Movement,'" I excitedly said.

"Are you ready for it?" she sincerely asked.

"As ready as I can get."

Mom then told Jason and I to get ready because we were going to the bakery to buy some double fudge chocolate chip brownies.

I loved my mom.

When I got to the old auditorium, I walked in and looked around. Much to my surprise, there were only six people there. I figured the others must be late and took my seat.

Twenty minutes later, and still no one else showed up. I saw Smiley sitting across the auditorium a few rows up. Then a black man wearing light-brown cackie pants and a white button down shirt came out of the side door and walked to the front of the auditorium.

He began, "Hello, everyone. Thank you for coming. I am Allen Minor. You are here tonight for the same reason I am—to fix the community. We don't have many resources with which to accomplish this goal, but we are determined. Because we have determination, we are bonded together and unified as a system. When you have unity in a common enterprise, you are bound to succeed."

I listened to him speak and was fascinated with his articulation.

He continued, "For years, the government has been promising a better, safer, and cleaner environment with viable resources for us to live in. But for some reason, they couldn't fulfill that promise. I say now that if we want a better community, we have to take charge of the situation. No one is going to look out for us, but us."

He talked for a long time about making the community safer and better and how to do that.

As he talked, I didn't really see how my studying and how this knowledge I have accumulated would at all contribute to this group.

It was 8:15 p.m. when we disbanded that night. Allen asked for questions or comments. I didn't have any, so when we were dismissed, I quietly got up and walked to the door. As I walked out, I felt enlightened and determined.

Determined to better the community—anyway I could.

SEVEN

"Alright guys. Wish me luck," mom very excitedly said as she stood at the front door in her new high heel shoes and brief case in hand. This is when I got up from the sofa and walked to her. Chris and Jason followed my lead. There, we all embraced in one big hug. Jason then said, "Good luck."

I kind of felt sad even though this was a great opportunity for my mom. For all of us. Sad because I was going to miss not having mom at home with me. Somehow she sensed my sadness and asked, "Roger honey, what's wrong?"

I then sadly said, "I'm going to miss not having you around."

This is when mom sincerely took my hands and said, "Honey, there'll be plenty of time for us to spend together. I'm just taking this job so we can have more and live life better. Please try and understand."

"I do."

"Good honey. I'm cooking a special dinner tonight. So get your appetite ready."

"O.K."

She then pulled me close to her and hugged me again while soothingly rubbing my hair.

"You guys be good and watch the place while I'm gone."

"Yes ma'am," I slowly said.

"Chris, you're in charge. You guys listen to your brother. There are packed lunches for you in the refrigerator. Bye, guys."

With that, she was out the door.

We all stood there for a second.

Silent.

We all thought the same thing. We miss mommy.

Suddenly, without warning, Chris announced, "Last one to the sofa's a rotten squirrel." We all darted for the couch, but I was not fast enough. Chris and Jason got the couch and because it wasn't big enough for three, I had to sit on the floor.

This is when I began to whine, "Come on guys. I was on the couch before mom left. I want my place back."

Then Chris said, "But you're too slow. So that makes you a rotten squirrel."

Not only that, but they were hogging the remote. They were watching the news while the cartoons were on.

It wasn't fair.

But then again, what was?

Around mid-day was lunch time. I couldn't stop thinking about mom and missing her more and more. We ate our lunches in the living room and watched T.V. After we were done, Jason got up and said, "I'm goin' to sleep with the fan on. Don't bother me."

He was right. It was extremely hot that day and the best place to be was in front of the fan.

When Jason got to his room and closed the door, Chris very nonchalantly asked, "How about a little game of one on one?"

I very excitedly said, "You're on."

I went into my room and grabbed the basketball and we headed out the door.

When we got outside, we saw some older kids at one end of the court playing and the other end was empty. We raced to the empty one. When we got there, I was so out of breath, I had to wait and catch my breath for a minute.

Then Chris very jokingly said, "Don't be there forever."

This is when I said, "I want to play HORSE," knowing this was a mistake because Chris was an expert shooter.

This is why he was the star of his basketball team.

He then said, "Have it your way, munchkin," as he took his first shot from the three-point lane. It went in.

"So what's up with you and what's her name?" I proddingly asked and took my shot from where he shot his. It missed.

He said, "What's her name's name is Carolyn and we're very serious about each other if you must know." He shot his second shot. It went in.

"Don't you think it's kind of dangerous you being involved with a white girl and you know those people don't like you?" I inquiringly asked as I took my second shot. It missed.

"Look we don't care what anyone thinks. We're in love. When you have love, nothing else matters." He shot another three-pointer. It went in.

"I'm just saying, don't you think it's a little dangerous." I took my third shot. It missed.

"Of course, it's dangerous. I'm not denying that. But then again, what isn't?" He shot from the side three-point lane. It went in.

"What isn't dangerous is you doing the right thing and leaving that girl alone. She's nothing but trouble. I shot the same shot he did and missed.

"Alright, I'll be careful. But I'm not gonna leave her alone. No chance of that happening. Isn't this an 'S' for you?"

"Yeah, it is. I didn't think you were keeping track."

"Well, get ready to say goodnight," he said as he backed up to mid—court. Suddenly, he came running down the court, then leaped in the air and gracefully dunked the ball. He then jeeringly looked at me and said, "Beat that."

I knew I didn't have a chance to do half of what he did so I said, "That's an 'E'."

Chris then excitedly said, "You're not even going to try?"

I said, "Naw, you won. Let's just go back in the house. Besides I'm kind of tired and I want to take a nap."

I was actually very tired.

When I awakened, I heard the sound of mom's voice talking in the kitchen. Also there was an aroma, which I did not recognize, that I smelled. But it smelled very good! I got up and went to the kitchen. When I got there, mom was there and Chris and Jason were sitting at the table. This is when mom said, "Roger honey, you're just in time for dinner. I was just telling your brothers about the new job."

I went and took my seat. Mom then began fixing the plates. We had fried shrimp, spaghetti, green peas, and biscuits.

Oh, it was good!

After dinner, we were all very full so we decided to leave the dishes for in the morning.

That night, I laid in bed with a full stomach and thought about me and Chris's conversation that day. I knew he was wrong, but what could I do? This is when I prayed to God. I prayed that He would let Chris see the light. Then I turned over on my side and wondered if God heard me.

We'll see.

EIGHT

I woke up to the sound of the T.V. in the living room. It was extremely hot that morning. Not only that, but I had a terrible pain in my stomach. I was very hungry. Yep, it was going to be one of those days.

I got up and walked to the living room to find Jason watching T.V. Mom had already gone to work and Chris was gone too. Without saying anything to Jason, I walked to the kitchen to get something to eat. I know mom cooked breakfast before she left.

When I got to the kitchen, there was no food on the stove. So I yelled, "Jason, where's breakfast?"

Jason then nonchalantly said, "You're too late. The early bird gets the worm—or in this case, the breakfast. You overslept again. It's time for lunch."

"Well, what's for lunch? I'm starving."

"Mom left some sacked lunches in the fridge. Chris is out and said he won't be back until tonight."

I grabbed a sack out of the refrigerator and the container of Kool-Aid. I then got a cup from the cabinet and sat down at the table. I poured a glass of Kool-Aid and then began digging in my sack.

Let's see. An orange. A peanut butter and jelly sandwich. Potato chips and cookies.

Not the most elaborate meal, but it'll have to do.

As I was washing down the last bit of my Kool-Aid, it hit me. I hadn't studied in a while. Right then and there I had my day planned—to study in my room until mom got home. I went to my room and closed the door.

When I got to my room, I opened the drawer with my books and searched until I found it. A book about the teachings of Dr. King and non-violent action.

As soon as I opened the book, I didn't read two words until I closed it back. I wanted to study, but it was too hot! There was no way I could study in this heat. I put the book back in the drawer and went to the bathroom to take a shower.

When I walked in, the first thing I noticed was the toilet seat was up.

Chris!

Whereas I was going to get mad, for some reason I didn't. I just put it down.

It's not a big deal.

I then took my shower and got dressed.

After I got dressed, I went to my room. I sat on my bed and thought, "There's gotta be a way to beat the heat." I then decided to go to the court and shoot some hoops. I grabbed my ball and headed for the door.

When I got out there, I saw the same older kids that I always see playing at one end of the court. At the other end was Trevor. I darted across the street to Trevor.

When I got there, I very excitedly said, "Hey, what's up buddy?"

He then replied, "Oh, not much. Just trying to beat the heat."

"I hear you."

Trevor then asked, "Wanna play HORSE today?"

I said, "Naw, it's too hot."

"That's no lie. So, what do you wanna do?"

"We could just chill."

"I couldn't think of a better idea."

"Let's sit over here," I said motioning to the sidelines.

"So, how's the group thing coming?" asked Trevor.

"Aw, it's alright. But it's not at all what I expected. It's a little boring. I have a meeting tonight. Wanna come?"

"Naw, that's not my type of thing. But thanks anyway. You know, school starts in two weeks," Trevor said.

"Yeah, I can hardly wait."

"But won't the group effect your school work."

"Naw, I'll manage."

"How's your mom?"

"She's doin' alright. She just started a new job. She says it's going to open up a lot of doors for my brothers and me. It's my brother I'm worried about—Chris. He's dating a white girl and they think they're in love.

"What's wrong with that?"

"Nothing really, except for the fact that her family and the whites in that part of town don't like Chris being over there or with her. I keep telling him to leave her alone. But he's so pig-headed, he just keeps going over there. I got a bad feeling about this."

"You know, the more you worry, the worse it gets. He'll wake up one day and see that she's not good for him."

"I just hope sooner than later."

"Hey, you wanna go get some ice cream? I'm starved." Trevor excitedly asked.

"Yeah, but this time is my treat."

We walked to the store and got ice cream. I didn't see Smiley today and didn't know if I wanted to or not. We ate our cones in silence while walking back to the court. Once we got back to the court, we were both done eating. He then said, "Alright, I'll see you later."

I then said, "Alright, see ya." Then we parted ways.

There was not much else to say.

I was watching T.V. with Jason when mom suddenly came through the door. Immediately, I jumped up to greet her. I ran to her and gave her a big hug.

"Roger honey, did you miss me much?"

I said, "Yeah."

She didn't know how much.

"Honey, I know your meeting is tonight, so I decided to come home a little early and cook so you can eat dinner before you leave."

"Thanks mom."

"Jason, set the table honey."

"Yes ma'am," Jason sluggishly said.

"Where's Chris?" mom asked.

"He's at his girlfriend's house," Jason replied.

"Well, I guess he'll just miss this good dinner," mom said.

"What are we having?" I excitedly asked.

"Tonight we're having meatloaf, mashed potatoes, and green beans. Now go wait in the living room and watch T.V. while I cook dinner."

I ran to the sofa and jumped in the seat. I picked up the remote and turned to the cartoons. Here I had the remote to myself for a change, I was going to eat a good dinner, I had a meeting tonight, and what's more, Chris wasn't around to bother me.

This was awesome!

We were about to eat dinner at 5:30 p.m. when Chris came strolling in.

Well, so much for that peace of mind.

"Chris, we're just about to start eating dinner, honey. Go wash your hands," mom said.

Chris then very conceitedly replied, "My hands are already clean."

"Christopher Michael Williams, if you don't go wash your hands right now... "

"Alright, alright."

"Hey Roger," Chris jeeringly said, "did you leave the toilet seat up again?"

"Leave me alone, Chris!"

Chris then threw me a smile and then stumbled down the hall to the bathroom. We waited for him and when he came back, he sat in his seat. Mom then said grace and we ate. It was delicious!

As soon as we were done, I took a shower and got dressed. Then mom walked me to the door and said, "Be careful." I then gave her a hug and left.

I didn't want to be late.

Today I decided to take the short cut to the old auditorium to save time. When I got there, I walked in and saw that the meeting had already started. I took my seat in the very back row. The same guy who spoke last time was speaking again. I tried to focus, but it was so boring, my mind began to wander. All I could think about was mom's new job, Chris and his girlfriend, and the fact that school started in two weeks. Every now and then, I would try and regain focus and listen to what he was saying, but when I did, I found myself drifting again. The next time I regained focus, I heard him say, "Any questions or comments?" I certainly didn't have any because I didn't know what he talked about. So as soon as we were dismissed, I quietly got up and walked to the door. I was very disappointed in myself.

But then again, disappointment was a factor that dominated my life.

But what else could I do but to live with it.

NINE

Here I was in a different city with my family altogether with me. Chris is doing great in school and about to go to college. Jason is also doing well with his grades and will follow in Chris's footsteps. Mom's new job is supporting us all and we can afford more luxuries. Me, I'm doing great in school and I have lots of friends. Not only that, but I get to study as often as I like.

Then I woke up.

I awakened to see Jason standing by my bed pushing my arm and calling my name.

"Roger, wake up. You're going to be late for school."

Here was a conflict.

I didn't want to be late for my first day of school, but at the same time, I wanted to go back to sleep.

I made my decision.

I hopped out of bed and went to the bathroom to wash up. Sure enough, the toilet seat was up again. But I didn't get mad.

I just let it down.

After my wash up, I went to my room and got dressed. After I got dressed, I grabbed my backpack and went to the door. Jason was there waiting on me.

Chris was already gone.

And mom had already gone to work.

I wanted to get something to eat before we left, but I didn't want to be late.

Then, almost as if Jason read my mind, he said, "Come on, you can eat breakfast at school."

Then we left.

When we got to school, the halls were packed. I saw lots of faces—some I didn't recognize and some I did.

This is when Jason said, "Alright bro, see ya later. I gotta get to my first class."

Then he disappeared in the crowd.

Then I saw Trevor.

I walked over to him and tapped him on the shoulder. He turned around fast and saw me.

He then happily said, "Hey, what's up?"

I then just as happily replied, "Nothin' man."

We then slapped fives and he said, "I don't know anyone here, but you."

I then said, "I'll let you meet some of my friends. But right now, I gotta get to class. I don't want to be late."

"I hear you."

"Alright man, I'll see you at lunch."

"Alright, I'll be there."

Then I turned around and headed for my first class.

I hoped today would be a good day.

When I got to class, I walked in and saw three of my friends from last year sitting in the back of the class. I walked back there to join them.

As soon as I sat down, we began talking.

"Hey Raj, did you get an inch taller?"

Then another one, "Is that a mustache coming in?"

Finally, the last one spoke up and said, "Naw, he just looks older cause he's stressed—with the death of his dad and all..."

I'm sure he meant no harm, but I couldn't take it. I blew my top.

I very excitedly exclaimed, "Hey man, why don't you talk what you know?"

He then very quickly and apologetically replied, "Sorry, I didn't mean to..."

"Just forget it!"

And with that, I was up and moved to the other side of the room.

Alone.

Then the teacher walked in and introduced himself. He began talking and I began drifting. My worries about Chris began to resurface. Then I began to think about mom's new job. How reliable was that? What if she got laid off?

What then?

Then I began to think about daddy.

Daddy why couldn't you have done what mom said and not try to be a hero? You would be here today.

I miss you.

Then I began to think about what my friend said about the stress from daddy's death making me look older.

Was this true?

If it didn't make me look older, it certainly made me feel older. Before long, it was time to dismiss. I hadn't heard a word the teacher said.

Also it had seemed like I had been there a very short time.

My, how time flies when you're concentrated on your worries.

At 12:00 p.m. the bell rang and it was time for lunch. I was extremely hungry from missing breakfast, and I was so looking forward to indulging in my lunch. Without hesitation, I very quickly made it to the cafeteria.

But then I had to stand in line.

When I finally got to the counter, I saw that we were having pizza, salad, and fruit cocktail. I quickly took my tray and began to look for a table.

I was so hungry.

Then I saw the same three guys from class earlier. They saw me and said, "Hey Roger. Over here. We saved you a seat."

But I was still angry so I very snappingly said, "No thanks."

Then I saw Trevor sitting in the back of the cafeteria by himself. I went to join him.

When I got there, he was very glad to see me and said, "Hey man."

I then replied, "What's up?" and took my seat.

He then quizzically said, "I thought you were going to bring your friends over so I can meet them. Where they at?"

"Oh, they're not my friends anymore. They're just a bunch of jerks. Forget about 'em."

"If you say so."

"So how do you like it here?"

"Well the classes are a little boring..." "And it's hard to make friends here..." "And the girls here won't like you unless you're already popular."

"Anything else you want to add to that list?" I jokingly asked.

"I mean it's not that bad, but it could be a lot better."

"I hear you."

"So, how's your mom's new job going?"

"It's going O.K., I guess. I just hope she doesn't get laid off."

"Yeah, that would be bad. How's your brother?"

"Oh, Chris is still Chris—as pigheaded as ever. He won't listen to me."

"He'll come around. But in the meantime, you need to stop worrying. When you worry it makes things worse."

"I wish I could stop."

With that, I got up from the table and went to the trash can to throw the rest of my half-eaten meal away. I was so distraught with worry, that I actually forgot how hungry I was and only ate half of my meal.

My worries dominated the day making it a very gloomy and dismal one.

When the bell rang at 3:00 p.m., and it was time to go home, I never felt happier. I found Jason and we walked home.

On the way home, we saw Smiley and passed right by him. Neither of us said a word to him.

When we got home, Chris was there sitting on the couch watching T.V. The first thing he said was, "Did you learn somethin' today, Roger?"

"Stop it, Chris," I replied.

"You mean they didn't teach you how to let the toilet seat down when you're done in the bathroom?"

"Shut up, Chris!"

"I'm just tellin' it like it is."

"That's not true and you know it. I don't leave the toilet seat up when I go in. It's you."

"Yeah, yeah whatever. Look mom said she has to work late tonight which means I get to play babysitter until she comes home. What do ya think of that?"

"I think you're a moron."

"Which is exactly why I want you to clean the basement. Mom says it's too much filth down there and she wants it clean. I would do it, but ya know..."

"No, I don't know."

"Well because I'm a moron, I'll have you do it. Can't have a moron do the work of a genius."

"Whatever. I'm going to my room to take a nap. Don't wake me til dinner's ready."

"Does that mean, no, you won't clean the basement?"

"The genius has spoken," interjected Jason.

"I'll clean it after my nap. I've had a really long day," I said headed to my room.

When I got to my room, I laid in bed and closed my eyes. As soon as I closed my eyes, I was dreaming. I had been dreaming for what seemed like a short time when I felt something nudging my arm. I opened my eyes to see mom standing there shaking me. Then I realized that I had been sleep for hours! I must've been really tired.

The first thing mom said was, "Chris tells me you've been misbehaving."

"No, that's not true. I just didn't do what he said was all."

"Well, I left him in charge, which means you have to do what he says."

"But mom, you don't understand..."

"No buts. Next time you do it, you're grounded. Is that understood?"

"Yes, ma'am."

"Good, now go eat dinner."

I went to go wash my hands and sure enough, the toilet seat was up.

I almost lost my mind!

Why was Chris getting away with so much?

I was furious!

Then I thought, "What would Dr. King do in this situation?" This is when I calmed down and began to say to myself mentally, "Non-violent, non-violent." Surprisingly enough, it calmed me down. I decided right there that from that point on, whenever something bothered me, I would mentally say, "Non-violent, non-violent." I then put the toilet seat down and went to dinner. When I got to the kitchen, Chris said something sarcastic to irritate me. But before I lost it, I thought, "Non-violent, non-violent."

It worked!

I was able to ignore Chris the entire meal. After dinner, Jason and I did dishes, then I went to bed.

I laid in bed and thought. This is just what I needed to get back into the groove of things. I now had a psyche technique to help me deal with anything. Then I prayed to God to let it work forever.

But how long was that?

TEN

The school year progressed, and as it did, my worries diminished. Mainly because of the new psyche technique I had and the newfound ability I had to residing to a more calm state when needed. Chris was still a pain and he tried me from time to time, but whenever he did, I just calmly told myself, "non-violent, non-violent," and he wasn't a problem. He was going to college next year and he'd really be out of my hair. He was still dating Carolyn and was the captain of the basketball team for a reason.

No one could play like Chris.

But on this particular Saturday, he came home with news that shocked everyone.

Chris came running through the front door and excitedly and out of breath, he exclaimed, "Mom, mom, guess what!"

"Christopher honey, calm down! What is it?"

"I just got the mail downstairs and I got a full scholarship to play basketball at SCU."

"Oh my God! Christopher, that's wonderful!"

I couldn't believe it. I was in shock.

"And what's more is, not only am I going to go, but I'm taking Carolyn with me. We're getting married."

Now I was really in shock.

"Christopher, you're serious, aren't you?" mom asked pleadingly.

"Honey, I'm proud of you, but you can't marry this white girl."

"Yes, I can and I will."

"Chris, I'm very proud of you. But marriage is a big step. Just think about it first before rushing into it."

"What's there to think about? We're in love. Besides it's me who's marrying her, not you."

"All I'm saying is don't rush into it. Just promise me you'll think about it."

"Alright, I promise."

With that I jumped up and grabbed my basketball and headed out the door.

I needed some air.

When I got outside, I saw Trevor at the court. The older kids weren't there today. I walked to the court.

"Hey man, what's up?" he said.

"The sky."

"I hear you. Wanna play HORSE today?"

"Naw, I got a lot on my mind," I said walking to the sidelines to sit down.

Trevor followed.

"So how's Chris doin'?"

"Which is exactly why I'm glad you're here, because I need someone to talk to about him."

"That's what I'm here for."

"O.K., you know Chris was dating the white girl. Well now he wants to get married to her."

"Wow! No kidding? How'd your mom take it when she heard?"

"She tried to talk him out of it, but you know Chris—stubborn as ever."

"Well just talk to God about it. And who knows, maybe things will work out for the best even if he does marry her."

"Yeah, maybe."

"Hey, check this out," Trevor said digging in his back pocket. He then pulled out a flyer.

"What's that?"

"O.K. Word is there's this new organization in town called 'The Revolution.'"

"So?"

"So this is not just any group. This is a radical group with radical ideas about lifting the black race."

"I thought that that's what 'The Righteous Movement' was about."

"You don't see. 'The Righteous Movement' is what you call passive aggressive. They're just all talk. But 'The Revolution' is more active. Kind of like 'The Black Panthers.'"

"So what does this have to do with me?"

"Everything! Don't you get it? This is where you really belong. You need to be more actively involved in the community instead of just talking. At first, I thought you'd fit in perfectly in 'The Righteous Movement.' But now I know for certain that 'The Revolution' is right for you."

"You know sometimes passive aggression is better than aggression."

"Yeah, but never is there a time when inaction is better than action."

"I hear you."

"Just at least take the flyer with you and think about it."

"Alright."

"Well I got to get home," Trevor said looking at his watch.

"Same here."

"Alright, I'll see you at school."

"Later."

With that, Trevor started walking home.

Me, I sat there for a while just staring at this flyer in deep thought. Should I at least look into it?

What would mom have to say about it?

It's at least worth considering.

ELEVEN

"Just think of the influence you can have in the black community by joining this group," I thought to myself as I sat in the front pew in church. Today I was in church because I needed a blessing from God. Whereas usually I don't bother with church because my focus is on other things like my studies.

Then he began.

I quickly told myself to focus and put everything out of my mind. My mission today would be to receive the word of God.

As he spoke, I actually listened. I didn't drift off and wander aimlessly in my mind about my worries.

The more he talked, the more empowered I felt. The loudness of his voice, along with the shouts from the other members of the church gave me a certain unexplainable peace of mind. As I got into it, I began to feel more like one of them. I felt like rejoicing God's name. Then my Amen's became louder along with my clapping and my focus was strong.

God was definitely in this church.

When it was time to sing the gospel songs, I sang loud with conviction.

Then the ushers came by to take the offerings. I had $10 so that's what I put in. To me $10 was a lot of money.

I knew God would be pleased.

After the sermon was over, and the last song was sung, I sat in my pew while everyone else was leaving. I was waiting on the pastor.

He saw me sitting there and he asked me what I thought of today's sermon.

In answering this question, I was as honest as possible. I told him that never had I been so focused and felt so at peace and close to God before.

He seemed very pleased.

Then I remembered what I stayed behind for—to seek advice.

"Pastor, I have a problem and it won't go away and I need your help."

"Well, anyway I can, son."

"O.K., my brother is dating this white girl that lives all the way across town. Which is fine, only the fact that her family doesn't like him because he's black and neither do the whites in that area. He keeps going over there to see her. Not only that, but now he's talking about marrying her."

"I see. Answer me a question. What was today's sermon about?"

"Oh, it was about the lost sheep."

"Mm, hmm. And what do you think it means?"

"Well, it means..."

"No, don't tell me. Talk to God and figure out what it means."

"But pastor, all I wanted was..."

"Once you figure it out with God, you'll see the light. Now if you'll excuse me I must be going now."

With that, he left the church.

And there I was all alone with nobody to help me.

But this is how it always was.

TWELVE

"Listen, I'm not telling you again. My final answer is no," mom said, brushing her hair in her bedroom mirror.

"But mom, this is exactly what I need to get known," I said pleadingly.

"You mean to get killed. This group is radical and violent. Now tell me, what do they have that your other group doesn't?"

"One thing they have that 'The Righteous Movement' certainly lacks is courage. This is what daddy had when standing up to those men. And this is the same thing that I have. Maybe daddy was right to do what he did."

She turned to me and slapped me hard.

"Go to your room and get ready for school. We'll talk about this later."

I ran to my room and slammed the door shut.

I didn't see what the problem was. Why couldn't I be a part of something with a positive cause?

There I sat on my bed wanting to cry. Not just about what just happened with mom, but everything.

Chris and his white girlfriend...

Daddy...

Where we were living...

Then it came to me suddenly—non-violent, non-violent.

I took a deep breath and said to myself, "non-violent, non-violent."

All of a sudden, I felt more at ease. My thinking was clearer and I was not so angry.

I even felt more motivated to clean my room and get to school. I cleaned my room and when I was done, I was ready for school. Jason was in the living room waiting on me.

Mom was already gone.

Then Jason and I left.

When we got to school, the halls were crowded. I told Jason I'd see him when school let out. And with that, I walked down the hall to get to class. I turned the corner and saw Trevor coming my way.

I quickly got his attention.

"Hey man, what's up?" I happily said.

"The sky and everything above it."

"But you know the sky's the limit."

"I hear you. Listen I'm gonna be late for class, but I'll see you at lunch."

"Alright man."

"Later."

As Trevor walked to his class and I walked to mine, I asked God to let me have a good day today. Then I walked in.

The bell rang at 12:00 p.m. for lunch. So far nothing bad happened and I was having a pretty good day. I was in the cafeteria with my lunch tray when I saw Trevor. He was sitting in the back at a table by himself. I walked over to the table.

"Excuse me, sir. Is this seat taken?"

"Depends."

"Depends on what, sir?"

"On if you're a Russian spy or not."

"And what does a Russian spy look like?"

"Well, let's see. They're tall, with mustaches, bald heads, and funny accents. But since you have neither, I guess you're cool."

"Right on," I said sitting down.

"So did you think about it?" Trevor said, biting into his sloppy joe.

"Yeah, I gave it a lot of thought and even decided I wanted to join. But when I talked to my mom about it, I brought up daddy and she got angry and slapped me."

"You probably hurt her when you brought up your dad."

"Yeah well, the slap hurt me more than it hurt her for me bringing daddy up."

"I can imagine. So how's Chris doin'?"

Silent pause.

"That good, huh?" Trevor said.

"My mom's the only one that can stop Chris from marrying this girl. All I can do is pray. Speaking of prayer, I went to church yesterday and prayed for Chris. And when it was over, I stayed behind and talked to the pastor. I asked for his help and he told me to reflect on the sermon he gave about the lost sheep which had an obvious message and was of no help. I tried to explain this and he then told me to figure it out with God, which again was no help."

"I think he means there's more to it than what you think it means and you have to figure the rest out with God to catch the full meaning."

"Yeah, makes sense. On a good note though, Chris has got a 4-year scholarship to play basketball at SCU."

"Really?"

"Yeah, I was surprised too. He announced this at the same time he announced that he was going to marry Carolyn. This news over-shadowed the good news."

"Just think when he graduates from college. He'll go straight to the NBA and he'll be rich, rich, rich."

"That's somethin' to look forward to." Suddenly, the bell rang and lunch was over. I hardly touched my food.

Then Trevor quickly asked, "Hey, you gonna drink that?"

He was referring to my unopened carton of milk. "Naw, go ahead."

"Thanks."

He grabbed it off of my tray and opened it and drank it hard and fast. He then stood up to take his trash to the trash can.

"Hey, did you want to play ball tomorrow?"

"Naw, I'm gonna be busy all this week because I have to write a 10 page essay. Plus I have 'The Righteous Movement' meeting."

"Although, where you need to be is in 'The Revolution'."

"Yeah, I know. But my mom doesn't see it that way."

"Have you ever thought about sneaking to meetings? Just say you're going to play basketball with me."

"I don't know. I don't really like the idea of lying to my mom."

"But what she doesn't know won't hurt her but will help you."

"I hear you."

"Just give it some thought."

"Alright."

"Alright, buddy. I gotta get to class. Don't get so caught up in your studies that we never play basketball again. And try not to worry so much. Everything'll be fine."

"Alright."

"Later, man."

"Later."

Trevor left and I went back to class. I took his advice and tried not to worry. When I did this, I found I had a more peaceful day. At 3:00 p.m., the bell rang and I found Jason and we went home.

When I got home, I immediately got started on my 10 page essay. I remembered what Trevor said about trying not to worry so much. When I did this, I felt more at ease and had a peace of mind. I ate dinner that night and Chris tried to irritate me the whole time. But it didn't work! I just ate and went to bed. Here was a peace of mind I had that worked better than the "non-violent, non-violent" psyche technique. Nothing could destroy this grand peace.

For now.

THIRTEEN

The school year progressed quickly. I hardly noticed how fast it was going by—just as I hardly noticed my worries. I found that by not focusing on my worries, I had a more peaceful year. I hadn't gotten into any confrontations with any of my school mates, at home things were alright, and Chris was not able to really get under my skin. Even though he was still dating and planning to marry Carolyn, I felt as if my not worrying kept things peaceful. The school year ended and now it was summer time. And this summer was going to be hotter than the last one.

I awakened to the sound of nothing.

Total silence.

It was almost kind of scary.

And I was extremely hungry.

I got out of bed and went to the bathroom. Sure enough, the toilet seat was up again.

Chris!

I used the bathroom and washed my hands. But this time, before I let the seat down, I stopped.

I thought to myself, "Why not let mom catch him so that he can get in trouble this time instead of me? Just tell her that Chris is the one leaving the seat up and he'll get in trouble for sure."

So I left the seat up and went to the kitchen. No one was home.

It was clearly lunch time, but I figured that since breakfast was the first meal of the day, then that's what I'll have.

I poured a bowl of "Captain Crunch" cereal and got a glass of apple juice.

After breakfast, I went and took my bath and then got dressed. "Let's see, what's on my agenda for the day? I could study here at home, I could go to the library and read, or I could go to the court and shoot some hoops. Well, I don't want to study here because it's too hot to study, I don't want to go to the library to read because it's too hot, and I don't want to play basketball because it's too hot. Looks like there's only one other option I have, and that's to stay here by the fan and relax.

It's just too hot.

I went in the living room, turned the fan on full blast and pointed it towards me, and sat on the big sofa.

Then I found the remote.

This was awesome! Here I had the entire house to myself with total control of the T.V., and the entire couch to myself for a change.

I turned the T.V. on and on the set was "He-Man and the Masters of the Universe."

Here I was with the fan, my cartoon, and more importantly—no Chris.

Just when I turned the channel to see if there was a better cartoon on, I turned to a station that had black men wearing black uniforms and black hats marching down a street. This interested me, so I watched more.

It was a documentary on "The Black Panther Party."

As I watched, I learned and my appetite for my interest in the black struggle grew. As soon as it went off, I went to my room to study on the works of Dr. King.

Not even this extreme heat can suppress the desire for knowledge. I went to my room and closed the door.

I stood in front of my book shelf—looking. There were many books on Africans, African-Americans, the great thinkers of the times, methodologies used by great leaders during the struggle... etc.

However, to me, there were none more fascinating than the works of Dr. King.

"Aha, here it is."

I found the book I was looking for.

I took my book and sat on the bed. I decided to start from the very beginning even though when last I was reading this book, I was 2/3 of the way through.

I held the book for a second and just looked at it. Then I began with the title, "Dr. Martin Luther King Jr. on Non-violence."

Just as I turned to the first page and began to read, my peaceful silence came to an abrupt end with three hard pounds on my front door. Just as I put the book down to go to the door, there it was again.

Then again.

I finally made it to the front door and opened it to see Trevor standing there out of breath.

I quickly said, "Trevor man, what's going on?"

He gasped for air and said, "It's Chris! They killed him!"

I heard what he said, but didn't comprehend it. I wasn't really in shock. I was just trying to comprehend what he said.

But I heard exactly what he said.

"What? What are you talking about?"

"Turn the T.V. on. It's on the news!"

I ran and grabbed the remote and turned the T.V. on. Then I turned to the news.

There was a woman reporter standing with her back to a sealed off area marked with yellow tape.

I listened...

"Apparently a one Christopher Michael Williams was here today visiting his girlfriend when four white men approached him with weapons. They then began yelling at him. This is when Christopher apparently tried to go past the men to get to where he was going. Then one of the men stabbed him in the back with a knife. This is when another man took out a gun and shot Christopher in the head..."

Before I could hear anymore, I dropped the remote and ran to my room. I jumped in my bed and began to sob very heavily into my pillow. Although, I couldn't hear anything, not even me crying. It was just total silence.

Just like when I woke up this morning.

FOURTEEN

I just lay there.

I was half-awake and half-sleep. I was dreaming, but the way I was half-awake was because I was still crying.

I dreamed about daddy and what happened in the restaurant. Only in the dream it was so real that it was almost like I was there. But where was I?

Where was Chris?

Then I found him.

He was lying in the street in a pool of blood. I reached out to touch him.

Then I woke up.

My awakening was sudden and disturbing. I heard my mom's voice yelling. As I listened closer, I heard a man's voice, but couldn't hear what he was saying.

Then my mom again.

"Isn't there something you can do? He is my baby."

Then I heard another man's voice say, "What do you want us to do? We have no suspects."

This is when I got up to go see who she was talking to. As I approached the living room, I heard my mom say, "If he were white, you'd have them already."

Finally, I reached the living room. I stood at the entrance and saw two white police officers. Then I saw my mom sitting on the short sofa. She was crying and looked very distraught.

And tired.

Then the officers saw me and then looked back at my mom and said, "We'll keep in touch."

With that they left.

My mom didn't see me standing there, but somehow she knew I was there.

She said, "Roger honey, come here." I went to her and hugged her tight.

She then grabbed my hands and said, "Honey, listen. I need you to be strong."

But I couldn't be strong. It was too much to handle. First daddy, now Chris.

But I said, "O.K."

By this time I was crying again too.

Then I heard Jason's voice scream, "Mom!"

I quickly turned around to see Jason standing there in tears. He ran to us and the three of us just embraced in one big hug.

Chris was gone and I knew it.

We all knew it.

But how to deal with it; that was going to be the challenge that I wasn't so sure I could meet.

FIFTEEN

The next morning, I awakened. The first thing that hit me was Chris.

Was it all a dream?

But the cold empty feeling inside of me let me know that it was real.

All too real.

I forced myself to get up and go to the bathroom.

When I got there, something appeared out of place. But I couldn't tell what.

Then I noticed it. The toilet seat was down.

I miss you, Chris.

We miss you.

Then I heard mom yell, "Roger, get ready for breakfast."

But I wasn't hungry. Although, I didn't tell her that. Instead I just said, "Yes ma'am."

I took my shower and got dressed. I felt refreshed after my shower. Refreshed because the water was cool as it hit my body. For a moment I felt like I was in heaven.

Where Chris was at.

I went to the kitchen to eat breakfast. I didn't see Jason. Or Chris.

But I did see mom there slaving over a hot stove. There were two plates on the table.

She saw me standing there and said, "Jason's not eating this morning. He doesn't feel well."

The second plate was for her.

But she never eats breakfast at home.

Then she announced, "I'm taking some time off. I just need time to think."

As she scrambled the eggs in the pan, I went to take my seat.

Then the kettle went off.

She poured her coffee and we had scrambled eggs, rice, toast, coffee, and orange juice.

Oh, it was good!

This was one of the best breakfasts I had in a long time. It certainly was a change from cereal.

We ate in silence.

Then she did dishes and I went back to my room.

Then I lay on my bed staring at the ceiling.

Thinking.

Thinking about when we were a family.

We were a family when daddy and Chris were alive.

I thought long and hard.

So hard, I fell asleep.

When I awakened, I found myself sweating profusely. It wasn't from the heat because I still had the cold chill in my body.

Just like when I woke up this morning. I got up and walked through the house.

My mom's door was closed so I supposed she was in there sleeping.

Then I went to Jason's room.

The door was closed. I stood there for a minute. All I heard was sniffles.

Then I went to Chris's room.

As I entered his room, I had the creepy feeling that Chris would be mad at me. Just as he always gets mad about me going through his things.

But what's the harm now? So I walked in.

His room was a mess.

I walked over to his desk and saw a bunch of papers. I began snooping around and rummaging through them.

What I was looking for, I really wasn't sure. But I'd find something.

Then I found a photograph of a white girl. This must be Carolyn.

She had kind eyes and was actually very pretty.

Then I found his acceptance letter to SCU with a full scholarship to play basketball.

There I held the photograph in one hand and the letter in the other. Then I looked at the photograph and said out loud, "It's because of you that Chris won't get this scholarship."

Then I tore the picture up and ran in my room and slammed the door shut.

There I lay on my bed and thought, "I just tore her picture up. But so what? That wasn't going to bring Chris back."

Nothing was.

She should be dead, not him. But nothing can reverse this now.

Hmmm...

SIXTEEN

Weeks went on with a terrible depression lingering through the house. There were many days of silence. But it was still summer.

And it was still very hot.

Too hot to be cooped up in the house all day long.

One morning, I woke up late as usual only to find mom gone. Jason was in his room with the door shut which is now what was routine for him for the past few weeks.

I decided to go to the court. Not to play, but just to chill and think. There was so much to think about.

When I got out there, the only person out there was Trevor. He was just sitting on the pavement and appeared to be in deep thought.

I walked over to him.

As soon as I got to him, I expected him to acknowledge me. Although, he didn't even look up. He just very sadly said, "I told you not to worry. When instead, had you have worried more, you would have tried harder to stop him and he'd be here today. I take some of the blame."

"No, that's ridiculous. There's no way you had anything to do with this."

"But now Chris is gone and there's nothing we can do."

"Maybe..."

"What does that mean?"

"We both know that Chris shouldn't be dead, but it should be Carolyn instead."

"Yeah, so."

"Maybe, just maybe it's not too late."

"I'm listening."

"Well, remember that group you told me about—'The Revolution?"'

"Yeah."

"Well, they're all about action against whites."

"Roger! Are you crazy? Are you thinking about what I think you're thinking about?"

"Listen, Chris was my brother. Besides an eye for an eye."

Trevor held his head down with his face in his hands for a minute. Finally I said, "If anybody asks, you didn't hear anything."

Trevor was still silent.

I got up and went home.

Was I crazy?

Yeah, crazy for revenge.

SEVENTEEN

I spent my next few days planning and scheming. Was it going to work?

Sure it was.

For Chris.

The plan was simple. I'd go to a few of the meetings for "The Revolution" so they'd get to know me better or at least get a feel for who I was. Then I'd rally them up with the story of Chris's murder at the hands of whites. I'd convince them to take up arms for such a racially motivated tragedy. Finally, we'd get the guns, go over there, and kill em' all.

It would work.

But mom can't know about any of this.

Which is why I'll tell her that the meeting nights for "The Righteous Movement" has changed to Monday and Wednesday. Then I'd simply sneak to "The Revolution."

Yes, it would work!

But I wanted to act as soon as possible. I'd tell her tonight.

"Let's see, today is Wednesday and mom gets home at 5:30 p.m. The meeting for 'The Revolution' starts at 7:30 p.m. I'll just go tonight."

God give me the strength to do this.

"Sure honey. I don't see anything wrong with that," mom said happily. I'm just glad to see you get back in the groove of things and not let what happened to Chris take you down."

"Thanks mom."

It was 6:45 p.m. when Jason, mom, and I ate dinner. We got done at 7:15 p.m. This gave me 15 minutes to get there before it started. Mom told me not to worry about the dishes, but to go on to my meeting and have fun.

Then I was on my way.

When I got to the building, I walked in.

They were already started.

I took a seat in the back and listened.

"I say to you brothers and sisters tonight, there is a revolution that will take place. And it will not be televised. We are here for a reason. The white man brought us here and took everything from us and profited from our labor. And then when they're done with us, they want us to go back. Well brothers and sisters, I am here tonight to say that we are here to stay. But while we're here, why can't we live in harmony and peace; or at least equal status to whites. I'll tell you why... because they don't want harmony and peace. They want war. So, let's give them war."

As I listened, I thought of the words of Malcom X, "By any means necessary."

The meeting rolled on for about an hour until the speaker opened the session up to open discussion.

I sat in silence and listened.

Then we were dismissed.

I went home and put my pajamas on. I laid in bed and thought and prayed. I prayed that Chris's soul was in heaven and that I was doing the right thing.

But right thing or not, what was going to happen was going to happen.

EIGHTEEN

Early the next morning, I jumped out of bed. I went and took my shower and cleaned my room. Neither mom nor Jason were up yet. I was up before them for a change. Why was I in such good spirits today?

Because of a new hope.

A hope to make things right.

I ate cereal and orange juice for breakfast. Then I did dishes.

Shortly after, mom woke up. I was in my room in front of the fan.

When I heard her door open, I got up and looked down the hall. I saw her half-standing in the hall and half-standing in her room. Suddenly she said, "Oh, it was wonderful. Now do you like coffee black or with cream?"

What was going on?

Had my mom lost her mind? Why was she talking to herself?

Suddenly, I heard another deeper voice say, "I'm a cream man myself."

Then my mom laughed and replied, "Stop being bad."

She slept with another man last night.

The nerve of her!

Daddy hadn't even been in the ground a whole year and here she is with some other man.

I have a good mind to go and straighten him out.

Homewrecker.

Instead I quietly closed my door shut and sat back on my bed.

I'll be damned.

About an hour later, I decided enough was enough. I got up, grabbed my basketball, and headed to the front door. When I got to the kitchen, there was mom in her nightgown sitting at the table drinking coffee.

Then I saw him.

A man wearing a robe drinking coffee as well. He very heavily favored daddy.

But this was no excuse.

Plus he was sitting in Chris's chair!

I couldn't take anymore. I blurted out, "Listen, you homewrecker, my mom doesn't need you and there's no way I'm ever calling you daddy."

He then very smoothly said to my mom, "I take it this is the charming one, Roger."

My mom then snapped, "Roger, that's no way to talk to an adult! And where are you going so early in the morning?"

"What do you care?" I snapped back. With that I headed out the door and to the court.

The court was empty. I went over there to play.

When I got there, I just decided to shoot around some.

I took my first shot. It missed. Then I shot many shots and they all missed.

Then I remembered when Chris and I played here and he showed me that dunk.

Should I try it?

Yeah, sure.

I backed up to mid-court and then came running down the court, (not half as graceful as Chris), and leaped in the air attempting to dunk the ball. But something happened.

I lost my balance and fell on the concrete pavement landing very hard on my arm.

I thought it was broken.

The pain was excruciating. So badly so, I began to cry.

Then I cried harder.

Soon I forgot about the pain in my arm and cried about Chris, daddy, this new man mom was with, where we were living, and whatever other problems I could think of.

I just lay there for a long time; not noticing the pain in my arm, but crying anyway.

It was peaceful here. I wish I could stay here forever. But I had other things to do.

NINETEEN

"We're going to the doctor and that's final. The worst he can say is to put a cast on it."

"Mom, you know I don't like doctors. How about if it's not healed in a week, then we go to the doctor."

"No, we're going and that's it. Not another word."

"This would have never happened had you not had forgotten about daddy and been with that other man."

I expected a slap coming.

Instead, she very soothingly said, "Roger, I need to meet people like Stewart. Your father would understand and be happy that I'm moving on and you should too."

"Stewart. His name is Stewart? That doesn't even sound like the name of a guy you're supposed to date."

"And just what kind of name should he have?"

"Mmm... How about um? Let's see... Roger."

"Oh really."

"Yeah, that's the perfect name."

"I see. Well go wake your brother up."

"Alright."

I went to Jason's room and opened the door without knocking.

He layed in bed with the covers over his head. I went to him and shook him.

He didn't move.

Then I shook him harder.

He still didn't move.

Oh God, not Jason too!

I shook him even harder and called his name.

Finally he moaned, "What is it? Let me sleep."

I then said, "Mom said it's time to get up. And don't forget the funeral tomorrow," as I walked out of his room.

The funeral would have been done, except mom kept prolonging it.

She wasn't ready to see Chris like that.

In a casket.

As mom was driving, my wrist seemed to hurt more and more. This was odd because this pain was sudden and instant. I then thought to myself, "It's probably just anxiety." Mom looked over at me and could read the pain on my face.

"Is it starting to hurt very badly?" she asked.

"No, I'm fine," I lied.

"Well, we'll be there in a minute."

Finally, we pulled up in the parking lot of the big building. Mom parked and I got out holding my wrist ever-so gently. Jason got out of the back seat, and we went into the hospital.

We walked down the hall to the elevator and waited for it to open. Then we got on and mom pushed the button for the third floor. As we were on the elevator, I started to get scared and nauseous about this visit. But that nauseous feeling could've just been that same queezy feeling I always get from riding the elevator.

Then we reached the third floor.

We then walked down the hall until we got to a wooded door with a glass window. On the window was the name inscribed Dr. Graves.

"Is this who we're coming to see?" I asked mom.

"Yes, he's going to examine your wrist."

Just the mere name "Graves" gave me chills. Then we walked in.

Mom went up to the nurse's desk while Jason and I took a seat. I could hear her say, "One o' clock appointment for Roger Williams."

The heavy-set lady sitting down then responded, "O.K., I've got him checked in and Dr. Graves will see him shortly."

"Thank you," mom said as she turned to come and join me and Jason.

Neither mom nor Jason said a word. And I didn't feel like talking either. But the good news was that there was a television that was on that I could watch. As I watched, I became less and less interested and focused as to what was on the screen.

All I could think about was Chris.

Then I thought more and my imagination began to go wild. I could actually envision Chris being attacked by these four white men that took his life and I wasn't even there.

Before long, a very pretty light-skinned lady came from out of the doctor's area and announced, "Roger Williams, the doctor will see you now."

I stood up and mom stood up too. This is when I said, "Mom, you have to let me do more for myself on my own. I got this."

"Are you sure?" she asked.

"Trust me."

Then she sat back down next to Jason.

I went back with the lady to meet Dr. Graves.

"Right this way," she announced.

Soon I came upon a room with a somewhat older man, who was obviously a doctor, standing at the door.

"Roger Williams?" he heartily announced.

"Yes sir."

"Come on in," he said motioning to a chair in the room.

I sat down and he sat down in front of me and said, "Now let's have a look at that wrist."

He very gently took my wrist and examined it for a little bit before he replied, "Yeah, it's broken. But nothing that a cast won't fix, and I can put that on right now."

He then got the cast material out of a drawer next to him and began constructing it around my arm.

"So, how'd you do this?" he inquired.

"Well, I was on the basketball court and I tried to dunk the ball like my older brother, Chris. But instead, I ended up losing my balance in mid-air and landing on my arm. You know, nobody could dunk a ball like Chris. In fact, nobody could play like Chris. He was the best! He had just gotten a four-year scholarship to play at SCU. But now that dream is destroyed because whites felt it necessary to take his life. He was dating a white girl. It should be her and those whites that are dead. If I had my way, I'd make sure they all were dead."

When I was done talking, I looked at Dr. Graves who was looking at me – with a look of pity.

"Well all done," he announced standing up.

Then I stood up.

"Would you do me a favor?" he asked. "If you could tell your mom I'd like to speak to her for a moment."

"Sure," I said. Then I turned and left his office to go get mom.

As she went to the back to talk to Dr. Graves, I took a seat next to Jason.

"Did it hurt?" he replied.

"Nope, I didn't feel a thing."

When mom got to the room, she walked in and he replied, "Shut the door, please."

She could see the tension in his face.

"Is he going to be alright? Everything is O.K., isn't it?"

"His wrist will be fine. But everything is not O.K."

"Well, what's wrong?"

"I'm worried that he may be suffering mental anxiety from his brother's death. I mean you should have heard the way he was going on and on about whites being dead."

"Are you insinuating that my son is crazy?"

"I'm just saying have him checked out."

"Thank you for your services, doctor. We won't be coming back here again," mom snapped.

With that, she turned and marched out of his office and then got me and Jason and we left.

TWENTY

Here it was. The day when I'd see my brother's body for the last time. Mom and Jason both had their showers, now it was my turn.

I went in the bathroom. I don't know who the last person out was, but the toilet seat was up. Neither mom nor Jason ever leave the toilet seat up.

It must've been Chris.

I let it down, took my shower, and got dressed.

Then we left.

I was so depressed, I had forgotten I hadn't eaten breakfast.

When we got to the cemetery, I stood in the shade for a while until it was time to begin.

Alone.

Then they were ready.

I stood next to mom with Jason on the other side of her as Chris was lying there in the casket about to be buried beneath the earth.

Then the pastor began.

As soon as he did, I drifted off and tuned out his words with my thoughts.

I didn't even realize how hungry I was, nor did I pay attention to who was actually there. I just stood there staring at my lifeless brother and thinking.

I tried to focus on the good times I had with Chris, but all I could think about was the day I would march into that white area with guns and take vengeance for my brother.

Then they started to lower him in the ground. This is when mom rushed to the casket and began to plead for Chris to get up.

It pained me to see mom like this. Though, as sad as I was, I didn't cry. I hadn't cried the whole funeral.

It was because I was done crying. I was ready to act.

TWENTY-ONE

I had been planning and plotting for quite some time now.

I was ready.

Now all I needed was the back-up of "The Revolution" and some weapons—guns.

I spent the entire day in my room thinking—perfecting my plan.

The only time I came out was for lunch.

It was 6:00 p.m. when mom made dinner.

Jason was still in his room. He didn't want to eat because he wasn't feeling well again.

"So honey, isn't your meeting tonight?"

"Yes ma'am."

"What kinds of things do you talk about there?"

"Oh, just basic stuff like the up-keep of the community, black awareness, and public interest concerns."

"Sounds like a handful."

"It is."

"I'm so glad you forgot about that 'Revolution' nonsense and decided to stick to 'The Righteous Movement.' My baby is a part of something positive."

"Well, I gotta go mom. I don't want to be late."

I got up and left.

I'm sorry mom.

When I got there, once again, the meeting was in session. I took a seat near the back and listened.

"As black folk, why are we here in America? Why are we here tonight? I'm here for the same reason you are—

because we need a positive change. Now however we get that change is up to whites. We can be either humbly granted that change through legislation and policy or we can forcefully make this change happen. And the way things are going now, it looks as if whites have opted for the latter."

Applause.

He paused.

"I know you all heard about the young brother that was killed some time ago by the hands of whites. I believe his name was Christopher Williams..."

Suddenly, I heard a voice out of nowhere say, "I know him." I looked around to see who said it. It finally took me a moment to realize—it was me.

Then I grew stronger and more confident as I stood up and loudly pronounced, "That was my brother."

Then I walked to the front. Even though the walk was not that long, it seemed like it took forever to get there.

Then I asked for the microphone.

"Yes, this was my brother. He had a very promising future as a great basketball player. He had just got accepted for a full four- year scholarship to play at SCU. Now his dreams are gone because whites felt it necessary to take his life because he was dating one of their kind."

What was I doing?

I didn't know, but I kept going.

"Now this group is about action. An eye for an eye and a tooth for a tooth."

This is when the speaker grabbed the microphone from me and said, "This is exactly what I mean. How much longer will we stand by as our brothers and sisters are murdered. We need to take action now!"

One person got up and left. Then two more followed. I waited.

Then the speaker asked if there was anyone else who would passively aggressively cater to the white man and leave.

No one else did, so he began again.

"Yes, everyone this is the old law an eye for an eye at its greatest respect. Now who's with me?"

The whole place went into an uproar of cheers.

Then he looked at me and said, "Be here Wednesday night at 7:30 p.m. so we can go over all the details."

"Alright."

"I'm sorry son and your name is...?"

"Roger. Roger Williams."

"Well Roger Williams, if it's a fight they want, then a fight they'll get."

And I was ready.

TWENTY-TWO

I anxiously awaited Wednesday. All I did Tuesday was sit in my room and think.

Then it came.

This was the first real step in preparation for my revenge.

"Alright mom. I'm gone."

"Roger honey, hold on. I've got a surprise for you. I'm coming with you."

"What?"

"I thought I'd go with you tonight and sit in with you to see what they're teaching my baby."

"Mom, nothing would make me happier than if you would come. But you wouldn't like it. Plus it's very boring."

"Honey, are you sure?"

"Oh, I'm more than sure."

She paused and thought; as if contemplating on coming or not.

I figured now was the best time to leave before she said yes again.

"Alright mom. I'm gone."

"Alright honey, have a good time."

With that, I was gone.

When I got there, everyone was just getting settled. The speaker spotted me right away. He signaled me to the front.

He then announced, "If I could have everyone's attention please. Tonight is a special meeting. You know that recently a young brother named Christopher

Williams was brutally murdered at the hands of whites. This is his younger brother, (addressing me), Roger Williams. Roger turned to 'The Revolution' in good hope and faith that we would be able to oblige him. Now we're a group of action. If the cops won't help him, then who will. We're going to march into that community and justice will be served. Anyone who has second thoughts or does not want to participate, the door is at the back."

One person left.

He then said, "I take it those who are remaining are demanding that justice be served promptly and quickly."

Applause.

"Tonight we're here to go over the details to stage this event."

"First and foremost we need weapons. Not like sticks and baseball bats, but guns. We need to set a time and a date. A perfect time is when they're most off guard. And who is the target? The target is every last one of them.

Because it might as well have been all of them that pulled the trigger on Chris."

"Where are we going to get the guns?" a voice from the crowd asked.

"It just so happens the Jamaicans up north have plenty of guns," the speaker responded. "We'll get those as soon as possible."

"The perfect date," he continued, "will be on a Sunday around 3:00 p.m. because they're just getting out of church and will be caught totally off guard. We will do this once I can get a hold of the guns."

The Revolution is here!

TWENTY-THREE

A week passed when I was informed at the meeting that he had the guns. The next morning, I woke up drained. It was to be this coming Sunday for it to take place. Since the last meeting and Sunday, I had been very quiet and secluded.

So much so, it scared mom.

"Roger, are you feeling alright?"

"Yes, ma'am."

"You know these past couple of days you've been awfully quiet. You're sure you're feeling O.K.?"

"I'm sure. Mom, are daddy and Chris in heaven?"

"Of course they are honey. And they watch over everything we do."

This made me feel uncomfortable. I then looked at my watch. It was 12:45 p.m. The speaker said be at the meeting house at 1:30 p.m. I then got up and said mom, "I'm going to the store with Trevor. I'll be back later."

"Alright honey, have fun."

I then stopped at the door, looked back at mom, and then ran to her and gave her a big hug.

"I love you, mom."

"Well I love you too. Where is this coming from?"

Without another word, I turned and walked out the door.

When I got there, they were all there and ready.

And so was I.

We got our guns and without much talk, we left. We concealed the guns in our clothing so as not to get caught by the police.

I put my gun in the front of my pants underneath my shirt. We walked and walked until we got there.

And the whites were there.

Without hesitation, the speaker screamed, "In the name of justice," and ran forward and pulled his gun out and began firing. Then the others followed—including me.

Whites were getting shot in the name of justice.

Then some whites came out of their houses with guns and began firing back. But then a girl came out hysterically running around because of the commotion. I recognized her from the picture I tore up in Chris's room.

It was Carolyn.

At last vengeance was mine.

I took aim and BOOM.

But there was a white person who was some distance away from me and who I didn't see because they were on the side of me and outside of my peripheral vision. I thought the shot that had been fired was discharged from my gun, but it wasn't.

It was his.

Before I knew it, I was on the ground.

My heart began to pump slower until finally it came to a stop. As the light grew more and more dim, suddenly I recalled a passage from one of Dr. King's speeches: "Brother, I may not get there with you, but I promise you that together as a people we shall get to the Promise land."

We're here, Chris.

EPILOGUE

My mom always was a strong lady. Yes, she cried when they buried me in the ground, but she didn't let it break her. First daddy, then Chris, now her baby boy. She had to get away from it all. She took Jason and moved to San Diego. There, they started over. She went to night school and got a degree and then landed a job as part owner of a great organization. Jason went through high school and graduated and went to college. I never fully figured out the underlying meaning of the parable of the lost sheep. But the meaning is simple. I was a lost sheep too. And now Chris and I have gone home to be with the shepherd.

AFTERWORD

When speaking of a revolution, a word that may come to one's mind is "extremity." It is the notion that a revolution incites extreme measures to bring about change to an undesirable state of affairs usually affecting a mass number of people in some way. In this sense, to revolt is to strike back against the oppressor.

It is my hope that the reader can relate to this underlying theme when reading this book. In this story, a revolution was taking place. The hostile interaction and events between black and white in this book are a constant reminder of the racial tensions and status quo of the way things are in America – even today.

The time setting for this book was in the 1980's; right in the aftermath of the Civil Rights Movement. The relationship between blacks and whites in America has always been very, very sketchy. We all know that the reason or origin of these ill-feelings manifest and date back to when blacks were first brought here on ships in the most undesirable conditions and forced into slavery.

But through hard fight and uprisings, things have changed. Blacks are no longer slaves – or are we?

Truth be told that blacks have come an extremely long way since the hardships of their ancestors – or have we?

I pose this question in viewing the living conditions for many African-Americans in the urban ghettos of this country. Also, in viewing the hostility and sometimes needless and tragic deaths that may incur from members of the police force to that of people of color simply just for being black. Then you have the factor of being black that unjustly influences many court decisions thus creating the disproportionate number of African-Americans in prison. There are many, many more examples I can cite of the effect of racism bestowed upon blacks in this country that insinuate that times in this country have not in fact gotten better. Whereas they have not gotten worse, I feel that they have not gotten much better.

Yes, we have more rights than when we started, but real change will not come from piece-meal legislation alone. There has got to be more open and honest dialect between black and white to really further the cause for change. As black people, we need to learn more about our ancestors. Not just the hard times, but the innovations as well.

And there were many!

Next, we need to set the tone for our youth. Have them learn the same and then they will have role models of color to look up to and inspire to be like. The negative stereotype that the media shows of blacks can be overshadowed with books. If we teach our children right, then they will be right.

It starts with us as adults, parents, teachers, and figureheads.

In the story line of this book, it was noted that the main character's father is who sparked the fire in him to read and study on the African-American innovators. I can relate to this very well because when I was the age of the main character, I too very heavily divulged into African-American thinkers and literature. My mother and father both helped to create this want and desire for the learning about my people. So, in this respect, the main character, Roger, was somewhat patterned and personalized as a reflection of me. And with this yearning and thirst for knowledge came a respect for myself because now I had role models who I could aspire and want to be like.

This is the reason that today I am college educated and the author of multiple books, one of which has been nominated to win the Eric Hoffer award and has also gotten the thumbs-up from Netflix to be made into a movie.

About the Author

James Mitchum Oates is the pen name of Brian Steven Curtis. He was born in Chicago, IL. on Oct. 19,1975. At a young age, he moved with his family to Kansas City, MO. He received his Associate's Degree from Penn Valley Community College in 2004. From there, he obtained his Bachelor's Degree in Criminal Justice/Corrections. He is the author of 8 published books, one of which is being screened for movie adaptation and has also been nominated to win the Eric Hoffer award. His marital status is single and he has no children.